Mother Grumpy's Dog Biscuits

(A True Tail)

Becky Wilson-Kelly

11-94   gift   28943

Henry Holt and Company · New York

For Payton

Published by Henry Holt and Company, Inc., 115 West 18th Street, New York, New York 10011.
Published in Canada by Fitzhenry & Whiteside Limited, 195 Allstate Parkway, Markham, Ontario L3R 4T8.

Library of Congress Cataloging-in-Publication Data
Wilson-Kelly, Becky.   Mother Grumpy's dog biscuits / by Becky Wilson-Kelly.
Summary: Master dog-biscuit baker Mother Grumpy hates dealing with
customers and is headed for disaster until friendly Ernest tries to help.
ISBN 0-8050-1287-7   [1. Bakers and bakeries—Fiction.   2. Dogs—Fiction.]   I. Title.
PZ7.W69955Mo   1990   [E]—dc20   89-24553

Henry Holt books are available at special discounts for bulk purchases for sales promotions, premiums,
fund-raising, or educational use. Special editions or book excerpts can also be created to specification.

For details contact: Special Sales Director, Henry Holt and Company, Inc.,
115 West 18th Street, New York, New York 10011.

First Edition   Designed by Maryann Leffingwell   Printed in the United States of America
1   3   5   7   9   10   8   6   4   2

other Grumpy baked dog biscuits
at her little bakery.
She baked all day and all night.

She baked biscuits in all colors,
all shapes, and all sizes.

other Grumpy's biscuits were the very best
dog biscuits in the whole world.

She used **only**
the finest ingredients.

She could bake biscuits so light and fluffy,
they seemed to float on air.
She could make them soft and chewy,
with delicious surprises in the middle.
She could make them crisp and crunchy,
with hearty flavor.

other Grumpy had a special talent
for baking biscuits.

In fact, she was talented right down to the
tip of her tail.

Every morning the aroma of fresh-baked
dog biscuits drifted out the door
of the shop and filled the air
for miles around.

ogs came from all over to try
a delicious biscuit.
They lined up for blocks outside
her little shop.

here was only one problem. You see,
Mother Grumpy was ... well,

Let's say her name suited her.

Even though she loved baking biscuits,
Mother Grumpy didn't like
waiting on customers.

They never make up their minds.

They never have the correct change.

They say stupid things like... "Good Morning" or "How are you?"!

If Mother Grumpy's dog biscuits hadn't tasted
so good, she might not have had
any customers at all.

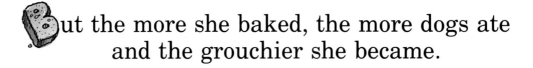ut the more she baked, the more dogs ate and the grouchier she became.

ustomers began to complain.

lthough she tried being nicer . . .

it didn't work,
and customers still complained.
In fact, business began to drop!

Then one friendly,
well-meaning customer volunteered.

She pushed him out the door and
slammed it shut!

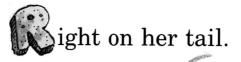ight on her tail.

"**B**urnt **B**iscuits!" she howled.
"My tail, my tail! . . . I'll never be able
to bake again!"

She held her paw to her forehead
and stomped around the room.
"How will I ever go on?"
she sighed.

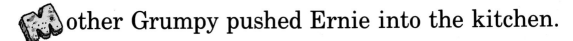Mother Grumpy pushed Ernie into the kitchen.

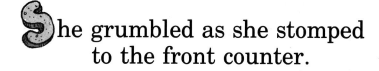

She grumbled as she stomped
to the front counter.

Customers are more trouble than a trip to the pound!

Well, guess what happened next! . . .

rnie's biscuits were the worst ever!

The flaky ones were doughy,
and the soft ones were mushy.
The crunchy ones were as hard as bricks,
and the chewy ones were rubbery!

Smoke poured out of the ovens,
and a horrible smell filled the neighborhood.

All the customers went home,
and Ernie and Mother Grumpy sat down, exhausted.

Suddenly, forgetting about her injured tail, Mother Grumpy had a brilliant idea!

arly the next morning
the aroma of fresh-baked,
delicious dog biscuits drifted
out the door of the little bakery and filled
the air for miles around.

ogs were lined up for blocks
outside the shop,
and when the doors opened, they all rushed
inside to try a biscuit!

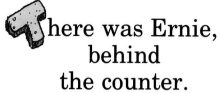here was Ernie,
behind
the counter.

He was happy. . . .

 he customers were very happy!

And Mother Grumpy was . . .well,

rumpy.

(But happy.)